The Adventures of Chaos the Cockerel

By Janis and John Lawrence

AuthorHouse™ UK
1663 Liberty Drive
Bloomington, IN 47403 USA
www.authorhouse.co.uk
Phone: 0800 047 8203 (Domestic TFN)
+44 1908 723714 (International)

This book is printed on acid-free paper.

ISBN: 978-1-7283-9401-5 (sc)
ISBN: 978-1-7283-9400-8 (e)

Library of Congress Control Number: 2019914929

Print information available on the last page.

Published by AuthorHouse 10/02/2019

authorHOUSE®

This is the story of a cockerel who lived in the country with his eighteen hens, four white and fourteen brown.

When Mr. Jones the farmer went to market to buy some hens he saw a very handsome cockerel with a lovely cream curly tail, chestnut brown feathers on his back like a saddle and a beautiful ruff round his neck of shiny cream feathers and a lovely big red comb on his head.

Mr. Jones got to the front of the crowd when the sale started and he called out to the auctioneer how much he wanted to pay for the hens and cockerel and after a while he was lucky as the other farmers who were hoping to buy stopped calling out their price so Mr. Jones paid the money and felt very happy.

Later on Mr. Jones went to his car to get the boxes he had brought to put the hens in and he gently one by one, put the hens into the box lined with nice clean straw. He then put the cockerel into another box and closed the lid. He took the box of hens to his car. A bus stopped at the bus stop bringing more people to the market and a little boy got off the bus with his mummy and while she was getting the pushchair off the bus the little boy went to the box with the cockerel in which Mr. Jones had left on the pavement and he lifts up the lid saying to Mr. Jones "What's in the box man"? and before Mr. Jones could answer, the cockerel jumped out and ran down the road.

Mr. Jones chased after the cockerel in and out of the shops and people stopped and stared and some tried to catch the cockerel by trying to put their shopping bags on his back, but still on he ran.

After a while he ran into a Builders Yard jumping over the stacks of wood and everyone laughed to see poor Mr. Jones all red in the face, puffing like a steam engine, chasing after the cockerel. Then just as Mr. Jones thought he would never catch the cockerel he saw the cockerel had run into a corner of the yard behind some bags of cement so Mr. Jones made a great effort to lean over the bags of cement to pick up the cockerel. The cockerel flapped his wings and tried to escape but Mr. Jones held on tight and, after a short rest to get back his breath, Mr. Jones tucked the cockerel under his arm and went back to his car. People clapped and called out "Well done - hasn't he had you on the run"!. Mr. Jones felt pleased with himself and opened the box, popped in the cockerel, put the box in his car and drove off home without stopping for his usual chat with the other farmers.

When Mr. Jones reached his farm, he made sure there was plenty of water in the bowls and he fetched some corn before taking the boxes into the chicken pen. The hens were so pleased to be out of the box that they ran around pecking at the corn and having long drinks of the cool water. The cockerel jumped out of his box and shook his feathers and he too had a long drink as he was very thirsty after running around the town.

Mr. Jones thought he too deserved a drink after all the chasing around so he went indoors to have his lunch and a short sleep in his chair by his cooking range as he felt so tired.

When Mr. Jones woke up he thought he would go to see if his hens and the cockerel had settled into their new home and he was so pleased to find them all happily scratching through the leaves to find worms to eat. He was overjoyed to also find six lovely brown eggs in the straw and he said to the hens "Thank you, you are good girls". He took the eggs into his cottage and put them in a bowl in the kitchen to show Mrs. Jones when she came home after visiting her friend in the next village.

When Mrs. Jones came home she too was very pleased to find the lovely brown eggs and she laughed at the story Mr. Jones told her of how he had chased the cockerel around the town.

Mr. Jones said it was time to give the hens and the cockerel their tea so he fetched the bowl of corn. Mr. and Mrs. Jones watched the hens eat and were amazed that the cockerel stood back to let his hens eat first and they knew that their cockerel was very well behaved - just like a gentleman.

The next morning as soon as it was light Mr. and Mrs. Jones heard the cockerel crowing "Cock-a-doodle-a-loo" "Cock-a-doodle-a-loo" and Mr. Jones said "It sounds as if the crowing is getting nearer". They looked out of their bedroom window and saw the cockerel proudly standing on the roof of the barn crowing and enjoying the warm summer sunshine. After a while he flew down from the barn and ran across the lawn as he had seen the birds eating their breakfast of the breadcrumbs that Mrs Jones put out every morning. The sparrows, robin, blackbird, blue tits, thrush and little jenny wren all flew away when the cockerel ran towards their breakfast crumbs and he was very naughty as he ate their crumbs. Mr. Jones fetched the bowl of corn for the hens breakfast and was amazed to see that when he said to the cockerel "Come along then and have your breakfast with your ladies" that the cockerel ran along behind him.

Later that day Mr. Jones found nine lovely brown eggs in the nestbox and thought to himself Mrs. Jones will be pleased and happy to have a fresh boiled egg and homemade bread for tea. Mrs. Jones you see made lots of lovely bread.

When Mr. and Mrs. Jones went to feed the hens at teatime they forgot to close the gate properly and before they could stop them the hens rushed out through the gate with the cockerel following along behind. The hens started to scratch around in the leaves on the lawn but as they were not harming the flowers Mr. Jones thought it would be a good idea to let them explore the garden. Mrs. Jones went in to make the tea and when she looked round the hens were following her. They even followed her into the kitchen and she was a little cross as she had washed the kitchen floor and the hens were making a mess with their muddy feet, so Mrs. Jones chased them out with the broom. The cockerel thought Mrs. Jones was going to hurt his hens so he flapped his wings and ran through the kitchen into the bathroom.

Mrs. Jones managed to chase all the hens out into the garden and when she went back indoors she found that the cockerel was in the bathroom. Mrs. Jones had been very busy all morning cleaning her house and the bathroom floor was slippery with polish and the cockerel slid around the floor and looked just as if he was skating! He flapped his wings and flew up onto the lavatory, then he lost his balance and fell into the lavatory pan and splashed about in the water. The poor cockerel could not get out and he started to crow, making an awful noise. Mr. Jones heard all the noise and rushed in to see what was happening. He laughed and laughed at the funny sight of Mrs. Jones waving the broom and the cockerel splashing about in the lavatory. Mr. Jones picked up the cockerel whose wings we're flapping so much that he jumped out of Mr. Jones hands and rushed through the kitchen, sliding all over the floor as he went, as he was in a great hurry to get back into the garden with his hens. When the hens saw him they gathered round and chuckled to him, then they all went back to their chicken pen.

Mr. Jones thought that there had been enough excitement for that day so he gave the hens and the cockerel their corn and went into his cottage to enjoy his own tea of a lovely boiled egg, home-made bread and cakes.

In the evening Mr. and Mrs. Jones were talking over all the funny things that had happened since Mr. Jones had bought the hens and the cockerel and they decided the cockerel should have a name. They chose the name Chaos which means to cause confusion and havoc and their cockerel had certainly caused that, both at the market and in their cottage.

The next morning Mr. and Mrs. Jones were woken up to the sound of Chaos crowing underneath their bedroom window and they wondered what adventures the cockerel would have that day.

Chaos and his hens had many more adventures, but you will have to hear of those another day.